bertha
and the Best Machine Competition
Story by **Eric Charles**
Pictures by **Steve Augarde**

from the original television designs by **Ivor Wood**

ANDRE DEUTSCH

First published in 1986 by
André Deutsch Limited
105 Great Russell Street London WC1B 3LJ

British Library Cataloguing in Publication Data

Charles, Eric
 Bertha and the best machine competition.
 I. Title II. Augarde, Steve III. Wood, Ivor
 823'.914[J]   PZ7

ISBN 0-233-97864-X

Phototypeset by
Kalligraphics Limited Redhill Surrey
Printed in Great Britain by
Blantyre Printing & Binding Co. Ltd Blantyre Scotland

Mr Willmake, the Manager of Spottiswood and Company, was in his office reading a letter. It was about a competition to find the factory that could make the most unusual toy.

"Our machines are good enough to enter," Mr Willmake told his secretary. "This is a job for Mr Sprott. I'm sure he could design an unusual toy. Ask him to come and see me, please."

Miss McClackerty rang the Design Office.

"I'll come at once," said Mr Sprott.

When he heard about the competition, Mr Sprott was very pleased. "I'm sure Tracy and I can design a toy that will win," he told the Manager. "We'll get on to it at once."

When he had gone, Mr Willmake read the letter again. "Mmmm. You know, Miss McClackerty," he said, "if we win this competition it will mean a lot of work for everyone in the factory."

In the Design Office, Mr Sprott and Tracy, his assistant, started work on the new toy. Mr Sprott drew the designs and made plans on large rolls of paper, while Tracy worked out all the difficult problems on her computer.

"This toy is not only unusual," said Mr Sprott, "but complicated. It will have to be made very carefully or it may not work."

"Which machine will you use to make it?" asked Tracy.

"Bertha of course," said Mr Sprott, "She is the BEST!"

Downstairs, in the factory, Bertha, the big machine, was making humming tops. Ted had oiled and cleaned her; she was looking smart and working at top speed. Working so quickly, in fact, that no one could keep up with her.

Roy was checking the tops as fast as he could. TOM took them from Roy, rushed them to the packing table and gave them to Nell to pack. Nell gave the boxes to Flo to stack.

Roy called to Ted at the other end of the machine. "Bertha's working too fast; we can't keep up with her. Can you slow her down?"

"No," shouted Ted. "Sorry. You'll have to find a quicker way of packing."

"I'm working as quickly as I can," complained Roy. The humming tops were coming onto the conveyor belt so fast, they were bumping into each other."

'Peep – Peep,' cried TOM as he tried carrying two tops at once. One slipped through his mechanical hands and fell on to the floor, spinning.

"That gives me an idea," shouted Roy. He pumped several of the tops and sent them spinning down the conveyor belt. "Don't touch them, TOM. Let them go by themselves."

'Peep — Peep,' said TOM watching them spin by.

As each top reached the packing table, Nell held open a box and let it spin in. Then she closed the lid and passed it to Flo.

"He – he – he! I'm being tickled," said Flo as she took the box.

"Who's tickling you?" asked Nell.

"The top. It's spinning inside the box and it's tickling me."

Everyone started to laugh.

Mr Duncan, the factory foreman, came by. He hadn't seen the top jumping into its box and he wasn't too pleased to find everyone laughing. "What's going on?" he asked, "This is a factory, not a fairground."

"Roy has found a quick way of packing the tops, Mr Duncan," Ted explained.

"Oh, has he?" said the foreman, grumpily. "Well, I don't approve. It looks more like play to me."

"But if I spin the tops into the boxes, we're testing and packing at the same time," explained Roy.

"Hmmm!" frowned the foreman, still not quite sure.

Suddenly, TOM pointed to the boxes behind Flo. The whole stack was alive with movement and swaying dangerously. TOM stretched out his mechanical arms and scooted across to the stack, but before he could get there, a box wobbled off the top and the whole stack came tumbling down on top of Flo.

"Oooooh," cried Flo, and Nell ran to help her. "It's the tops," she said, "They're still spinning in the boxes."

"This is your bright idea, is it, Roy?" said Mr Duncan.

Roy helped Nell to pull the boxes off poor Flo. "It shows that Bertha makes jolly good humming tops, if they go on spinning all this time," he said.

"Yes. Well, let's hope they stop spinning before they get to the shops," said the foreman, and stalked off, leaving them to rescue Flo.

Flo was still giggling under the boxes. "I hope she is all right," said Ted. They removed the last box and Flo sat up. "I've been tickled all over," she gasped.

The Manager was delighted when he saw the designs. "Splendid! Splendid, Mr Sprott. These should win us the competition. Let's get one made at once."

Upstairs, in the office, Mr Sprott and Tracy had finished the designs for two new toys. "I think these are our best inventions yet," said Tracy.

"Thank you," said Mr Sprott. He rolled up the drawings and tucked them under his arm. "I'll show them to Mr Willmake first," he said, "and then I'll take them down to Bertha."

Bertha had finished making humming tops, and Panjid was loading the boxes onto his forklift-truck, ready to take them to the dispatch department.

"Careful," Roy warned him, "We don't want those tops spinning again."

"I will be most careful," said Panjib, as he drove off.

Nell and Flo sat down on a packing case. "What's our next job?" Nell asked.

At that moment Mr Willmake and Mr Sprott arrived with the plans for the new toys. "I've got a job for you," said Mr Willmake, "Ted, do you think Bertha can make one of these?"

Ted studied the plans carefully and then nodded. "Mr Willmake," he said, "Bertha can make anything."

Mr Duncan came along, still in a grumpy mood. "You're not giving an important new toy to Bertha to make, are you?" he asked the Manager.

"The new Super Bumper and Presser machine will make a far better job of it."

Mr Willmake looked doubtful. "I'm not so sure," he said.

"Well, I am," said Mr Duncan, "As foreman of this factory, I say that the new toy should be made on an up-to-date machine."

"Mmmm. Well, I suppose I must agree with you," said the Manager, taking the plans from Ted and going off with the foreman and Mr Sprott.

"That new machine's no better than Bertha," said Roy.

"Of course not," said Nell and Flo together.

'Peep – Peep,' TOM agreed.

"You're right," said Ted, "And I am going to prove it." He went to the control board and started pressing the buttons. Bertha's lights began to flash.

"What are you doing?" asked Roy.

"I think I can remember those plans," said Ted. "So I'm programming Bertha to make one."

"Hooray!" shouted Roy, "Come on, Bertha, you show them."

Bertha's wheels began turning and her cogs meshed. 'Clink – Clank – Clonk,' she went.

Mrs Tupp came along with her tea-trolley. "Who would like a nice cup of tea?" she asked.

"Not just now, thank you, Mrs Tupp. We're very busy," said Ted.

"Nobody seems to want any tea this morning," said Mrs Tupp. "The others are all round that new machine waiting for some toy to be made."

"Let's have a look," said Ted.

The Super Bumper and Presser machine was working at full speed. Mr Sprott looked at his pocket watch. "Any moment now," he said.

A bell rang. The motor switched off and all was quiet. Faintly, from inside the machine came the sound of tinkling music. As it grew louder, everyone leaned forward to watch.

There was a gasp of admiration as a beautiful doll appeared, dancing down the conveyor belt. It skipped to the left and then to the right, its feet tapping out the beat of the music. It raised its arms above its head and twirled first one way and then the other. The music stopped and the doll gave a bow. Everyone clapped.

"Well done, Mr Sprott," said the manager, "You've hit on a winner, for sure."

"Thank you," said Mr Sprott, "I'll set it dancing again." He moved a small lever at the back of the doll. The tinkling music began again and the doll twirled and skipped and tapped to the rhythm of the music. Then, without warning, the music speeded up, and the doll jerked awkwardly, trying to keep time.

"Something's gone wrong," exclaimed Mr Sprott.

Faster and faster played the music; faster and faster danced the doll, until, suddenly, the music stopped. There was a small puff of blue smoke and the doll fell over.

"It can't have been properly made," said Mr Willmake.

"Perhaps we should have used Bertha," said Mr Sprott.

"We did," said Ted. "Listen."

From the other side of the factory came the sound of Bertha working.

'Clink – Clank – Clonk!'

"Is she making my doll?" asked Mr Sprott.

"Come and see," said Ted and led everyone back to Bertha.

Bertha was enjoying herself. 'Clink – Clink – Clank – Clank – CLONK!'
she went and 'Wheeeeez! Clonk!' and stopped. The sound of music came
from inside the big machine.

"Here it comes," shouted Roy as the music grew louder.

Out of Bertha marched a brightly uniformed bandboy doll. He performed a quick dance, threw a baton into the air and caught it.
He gave a smart salute, stepped on to the moving conveyor belt and rode down it,

twirling the baton in one hand and raising his hat with the other.

Everyone cheered.

"That's wonderful," said the Manager.

"Even better than the one I designed," beamed Mr Sprott.

Ted patted Bertha. "That," he said, "is because it was made by THE BEST MACHINE."